The Casebook of
Mysterious Morris

JOHN MELIA

authorHOUSE®

AuthorHouse™ UK Ltd.
500 Avebury Boulevard
Central Milton Keynes, MK9 2BE
www.authorhouse.co.uk
Phone: 08001974150

First published by AuthorHouse 5/18/2010

ISBN: 978-1-4520-1809-6 (sc)

This book is printed on acid-free paper.

Mysterious Morris

AND THE RAID ON ICEPAK

Mysterious Morris is biding his time,
Watching the clock, awaiting its chime,
The ten o'clock signal for Mrs Molloy,
To hug him and whisper, 'Now be a good boy,'
As she carries him out to his basket before,
She turns off the light switch and closes the door.

Alone in the kitchen as dark as a cave,
Mysterious Morris yawns and then savours,
The moist meaty morsels that Mrs Molloy,
Always leaves in his bowl for her Mo to enjoy.
And then down to business, there's no time to waste,
He left clear instructions that they should make haste,
To meet him inside after putting-out time,
There's hard work ahead and a difficult climb.

At that very moment they start to appear,
The cat flap swings open and, yes, they're all here.
There's Conker McGuinness and Footpad Magee,
And Algernon Flappit the tabby makes three.
They all know the plan, so a wave of Mo's paw,
And they're off toward Icepak, the new superstore.
With careful research and cunning disguise,
Mysterious Morris has sniffed out the prize.

Along the back entry and under the fence,
Where Algie gets stuck, since he's no common sense.
Then over the car park and right round the back,
The journey's completed, it's time to attack.
Mo signals the window high up in the wall,
A vertical climb and a horrible fall.
But Footpad just winks and says, 'Stand aside boys,
We need to get in without making a noise.'

Then he's off like a rocket, scaling the drop,
Moving so quickly in order to stop,
Only when within reach of the small window ledge,
With a sigh of relief his claws find the edge.
He knows what to do, the scheme's been rehearsed,
Inside, down the staircase in silence, but first,
Check out where Flint, the security man,
Is snoozing, or else he could ruin their plan.

In no time at all Footpad opens the latch,
Releasing the bolt which releases the catch,
On the small wire gate at the rear of the store;
The gang is inside keeping low to the floor.
They know the direction and move through the shop,
In seconds they make it then, sniffing, they stop.
A wonderful smell, every cat's fondest wish,
A counter containing a pile of fresh fish.

There on the ice, a cat's fishy delight,
A heavenly banquet from last to first bite.
Salmon and trout, hake, bass and bream,
Herring and mackerel in moonlight all gleam,
As four friends prepare for the hard work ahead,
A crime to commit, many mouths to be fed.
Conker is first to begin as he sinks,
His teeth in a salmon, then spots Mo and winks.

'Come on lads,' says Morris, 'There's forty six fish,
To shift from this counter into someone's dish.'
So, hauling and dragging and carrying too,
Time after time the four furry crew,
Make off with the fishes, away through the door,
Returning each time to collect even more.
Over the car park, around by the back,
Of the bin shed, the cats pile their fish in a stack.

It grows until Icepak's fish counter is bare.
Mo grabs the last herring and takes a last stare.
Then just as he's making his way off the shelf,
A torch beam arrests him, it's Bill Flint himself.
Mo thinks of escape but there's nowhere to go.
He's cornered. Flint whistles his dog, Pitbull Joe.
But out of the darkness a noise emanates,
The sound of bold Morris's gang of good mates.

From one side a hissing as Conker creeps in,
Behind, Footpad growls just to add to the din.
It's pitch black as Algernon howls even more,
A terrible, hideous noise from the floor.
Flint spins with his torch beam and gasps in surprise,
As light catches pair after pair of green eyes.
Unable to see, Pitbull Joe runs away,
Forsaking his master, confused by the fray.

'Thanks lads,' Morris pants as they run from the store.
'Now, Algie, the signal, let's give them all more.'
On cue Algie howls and the four sit beside,
The mountain of fish as a dark, seething tide,
Of whiskers and fur, and purring big eyes,
Seeps forward and gazes in joy and surprise.
Mo's feast piled before them, the legion of cats,
Who, homeless, live under the tower block of flats.

The sad, the unwanted, abandoned and old,
The forsaken, defenceless, all shiver with cold.
Each uncared-for cat whom fate cruelly sends,
Survives thanks to Morris and his artful friends.
When everyone's fed and the night's work is done,
The robbers bound homeward as dawn brings the sun.

And into the kitchen comes Mrs Molloy;
'Oh Morris,' she smiles, 'you lazy big boy.'
He blinks at her from where he lies on the chair,
And purrs to himself as she ruffles his fur.

....

Mysterious Morris

AND THE BLACKBERRY DRIVE POISONER

Standing some distance from Blackberry Drive,
The old railway station and platform survive,
From days long ago when the trains ran on time,
And motor cars hadn't yet quite reached their prime.
And standing in front of this derelict place,
An old water butt occupies the same space,
It did when the station first opened and saw,
Its very first train back in 1904.

In hiding beside this disused railway line,
Mysterious Morris is biding his time;
Watching the pool at the water butt's base,
That's commonly used as a cats' drinking place.
They come and they go as the evening wears on,
Pausing to lap from the pool every one,
Of the cats who are out on the prowl for the night,
But Morris needs proof that there's something not right.

As midnight approaches, it happens at last,
A dark silhouette in a raincoat creeps past,
The old station building, approaching the pool,
That shines like a glistening, moonlit black jewel.
From inside his raincoat the figure then takes,
A bottle of something whose contents he shakes,
Deliberately into the water below,
Then turns up his collar, preparing to go.

As Morris looks on with suspicious dismay,
The dark figure furtively hurries away,
Followed by Morris's narrowing eyes,
The raincoat was not a successful disguise.
There's mischief afoot and it calls for a plan,
But first he must find out as much as he can.
So, following at a safe distance he goes,
To prove to himself what he already knows.

Close to the corner of Blackberry Drive,
Live Ned and Veronica at Number Five.
It's been Ned's address for the whole of his life,
The past twenty years with his neighbourly wife.
His garden is always his pride and his joy,
Occasioning comment from Mrs Molloy.
'My goodness, your roses are beautiful, Ned.
You've got real green fingers, as I've always said.'

Year after year Ned has gardened and fussed,
The kind of good neighbour you know you can trust.
Held by all residents in high esteem,
But things with Ned may not be quite what they seem.
Silent resentment and bitterness that's,
Eventually turned to a hatred of cats,
Has grown in Ned's mind into licence to kill,
Any one of these feline trespassers at will.

Veronica's silent as Ned raves and rants,
'I'm sick of these cats always spoiling my plants;
Pooing and weeing all over the place;
I've run out of patience, it's just a disgrace.
If owners refuse to control their own pet,
I'll teach them a lesson that they won't forget.'
Thus neighbourly Ned became Poisoner Ned,
Preparing vile potions in his garden shed.

Next day a meeting is called in great haste,
By Morris, who now knows there's no time to waste,
If he's to stop Poisoner Ned in his tracks,
And save many cats from his murderous attacks.
So once again inside the old garden shed,
The company gathers with business ahead.
There's Conker McGuinness and Footpad Magee,
And Algernon Flappit the tabby makes three.

'All cats must be warned not to drink from that pool,'
Says Morris, 'Ned's cunning, he's nobody's fool.
Who would suspect such a neighbourly man,
Of carrying out such a dastardly plan.
I see now why so many cats from our street,
Have all become ill and unable to eat.
And should they keep drinking that poison, indeed,
In time Ned will kill them, his plan will succeed.'

'But how can we stop him from carrying on?'
Asks Conker, 'That pool by the station's just one,
Of a whole range of water holes cats always use.
We can't save them all just by spreading the news.'
'Indeed,' Morris answers and furrows his brow,
'Direct action's what we must take, and here's how.
Last night when I followed him home I found Ned,
Brews up the foul poison in his garden shed.'

'He uses a gas stove to boil the stuff up,
Then leaves it to cool in a dirty old cup.
It's time that we visited Ned's secret lair,
But first we must check to make sure he's not there.
And meanwhile we need to send out a command,
To summon all cats so a crowd is on hand.
I want Ned the Poisoner left in no doubt,
By cats will his downfall have been brought about.'

Friends in the district are soon all informed,
At daybreak Ned's lawn is to be cat-adorned,
And Black Burt the Shadow invisibly creeps,
Away to Ned's home where a vigil he keeps,
Waiting for Ned to step out of the shed,
And trudge up the garden on his way to bed.
A howl from Black Burt alerts Morris and friends.
On timing and stealth his dark plan now depends.

The back of Ned's shed has a hole in the wall,
So, through this the cats one by one squeeze and crawl.
With Burt in the tree on the lookout outside,
And Algernon, Footpad and Conker inside,
Now Morris crawls in, quickly looking around,
Then nods his approval, the answer is found.
The thin rubber hose is precisely the thing,
Connecting a cylinder to Ned's gas ring.

'Ok boys,' says Morris, 'let's get this job right.
Take hold of the pipe and get ready to bite.'
Needle-sharp teeth get to work on the hose,
Piercing the rubber, the gas to expose.
In seconds it's done, leaving Morris to shout,
'Right lads, let's get going, it's time to get out,'
As odourless butane continues to spread,
Throughout the interior of Ned's doomed shed.

As Morris had ordered, approaching the dawn,
A crowd of the neighbourhood's cats fills Ned's lawn;
Come to bear witness as justice is done;
For Poisoner Ned now his judgement day's come.
The cats run and hide at a wave of Mo's paw,
As day breaks and Ned appears at the back door.
The shedful of gas now stands lying in wait
Ready and primed to deliver his fate.

Preparing to boil up more poisonous brew,
He enters the shed, disappearing from view;
The signal for forty three cats to appear,
To watch and to wait, safely keeping well clear.
The seconds tick by and the tension soon grows,
Then suddenly, at last the wooden shed blows.
When Ned strikes his match, although hidden from view,
A blinding red flash gives the cats quite a clue.

The roof blows right off, landing two streets away,
The four walls are flattened, in splinters they lay.
And there, on all fours, in the middle crawls Ned,
With not a hair left on his smoke-blackened head;
A spluttering, smouldering, coughing, shocked mess,
With cardigan shredded and quite eyebrow-less.
Then stumbling and staggering, scratching his head,
He stands to behold his exploded ex-shed.

But worse is to come as the dust starts to clear,
A sight that strikes Poisoner Ned dumb with fear.
The crowded assembly of cats on the lawn,
All silently staring their vengeance and scorn.
Immediately Ned understands what's gone on,
And runs for the back door, in seconds he's gone.
With mission accomplished the cats all depart,
Happy to know that they've each played their part.

Close to the corner of Blackberry Drive,
The house that stands empty is Ned's Number Five.
He and Veronica fled that same day,
Never again to be seen down that way.
And Mrs Molloy said she found it quite weird,
That Ned and Veronica just disappeared,
Never suspecting, and failing to spy,
The mischievous twinkle in Morris's eye.

....

Mysterious Morris

AND THE UNEXPECTED NEW FRIEND

When Whispering Will came calling one night,
Mysterious Morris received quite a fright.
From nowhere Will's gaunt figure simply appeared,
Bringing bad news, just as Morris had feared.
In hushed tones the caller began to explain,
'I've come from my neighbours on Brownberrie Lane.
Not one of us cats will go out any more,
We're too scared to venture beyond the front door.'

Continuing his explanation in haste,
It soon became clear there was no time to waste.
A day never passed, so it seemed, when some mog,
Wasn't chased or attacked by a fearsome dog.
Such things never happened on Brownberrie Lane,
Till three weeks ago, Will went on to explain,
When Buttons Divine had been found by Black Burt,
Cowering in terror and quite badly hurt.

And then three days later old Zanzibar Joe,
Was attacked without warning while making his slow,
Laboured progress back home from his prowl in the park,
They knew without doubt this meant bite not just bark.
Next day was the turn of poor Mincy Maguire,
Left bitten and chewed like an old rubber tyre.
Then Claude Fancy Jones ended up at the vet,
As the nasty attacks became more nasty yet.

'Can you do something, Morris?' asked Whispering Will,
'I can't help but think that this mad dog might kill.'
Mysterious Morris proceeded to think,
Already convinced that there must be a link,
To the owner of such a despicable pet;
'I've never encountered a vicious dog yet,
Whose owner was not maladjusted himself,
Determined to harm his own dog's mental health.'

The following night as cats' minders all slept,
An urgent appointment with Morris was kept,
By Conker McGuinness and Footpad Magee,
And Algernon Flappit the tabby made three.
Soon Morris explained they were all up against,
A dangerous dog, unleashed and unfenced.
'A once-and-for-all plan we need for this hound,
Which means we must corner him on his home ground.'

Agreed on the first job, the friends separate,
To track down the home of this feared reprobate.
Farther afield they are sure they must go;
No dog of this nature lives close by, they know.
So, scouring the gardens, all four cats fan out,
Till Algernon summons them all with a shout.
The three others head for his shrill caterwaul,
And find Algie perched on a high backyard wall.

Far past the shops and beyond the canal,
He's tracked down the lair of the dread animal.
Massive head resting on paws, snoring hard,
They behold the huge Rottweiler down in the yard.
Then, creeping towards them appears a grey cat,
Timid and anxious and terrified that,
They might wake the monster from his sleeping lair.
Mo leaps to safe ground and they all join him there.

Smokey Sue tells them how, four weeks before,
This dog and his master, Syd Gutt moved next door.
Since then she's been housebound, too scared to go out,
Though she's heard of the nasty attacks round about.
The sound of the bolt on the back door is heard,
And there stands Syd Gutt in string vest and a beard,
With brown boots and camouflage trousers above,
A vision that only Syd's mother could love.

'Get out you,' he snarls as he kicks at the dog,
Then brandishes a black and white soft toy mog.
'Go for it, Buster,' he shouts at the hound,
Then drops the toy cat so it falls to the ground.
Pouncing, the rottweiler seizes the toy,
And rips it and shreds it as Gutt shouts, 'Good boy.'
Then drooling and foaming, it basks in Gutt's praise,
Lost in a mindless, obedient daze.

The friends bound off homeward, they're grateful to put,
A good mile or more between them and Syd Gutt.
'I still think there's hope for that dog,' Morris says,
'If he could be freed from that evil man's ways.
It's time for a plan, there are cats to protect,
And a shock for Syd Gutt that he doesn't suspect.'
By twilight next day his new plan is explained,
They'll liberate Buster and Gutt will be blamed.

'But what if you're wrong, and he really is bad?'
Asks Conker, 'If we set him loose he'll go mad.'
'It's men who turn dogs into bullying slaves,'
Says Morris, 'Once free, see how Buster behaves.
I just need the chance to convince him that he,
Can be a good dog and live quite peacefully.'
And so, with misgivings, the friends all agree,
To follow Mo's instincts, though reluctantly.

'Send for the strays and the ferals,' he nods.
'We'll transform the monster against all the odds.'
In no time at all, in response to the call,
A long line of cats sits on Syd's backyard wall.
Along the whole length of three walls of the yard,
Sat shoulder to shoulder, as if standing guard,
Is every conceivable species of mog,
Ready to re-educate the mad dog.

Rows of black points in the dark touch the sky,
Eighty six ears all assembled to try,
To help Morris succeed in his cunning new plan,
To mend Buster's delinquent ways if he can.
As down in the darkness, the dog starts to doze,
A whiff of fresh cat scent approaches his nose.
Lifting an eyelid, he cats a cold eye,
High up on the wall where the bricks meet the sky.

Hardly believing his own sleepy eyes,
He scans the whole length of the wall in surprise.
In unison, forty three cats start to purr,
While eighty six eyes all relentlessly stare,
At the dog down below, who in instinct reacts,
Beginning to bark before checking his facts.
Yelping and roaring, he leaps up and down;
On top of the wall Morris stares with a frown.

The back door is opened, Syd Gutt rushes out,
Instantly giving his pet such a clout,
With the toe of his boot, Buster yelps with the pain,
His master retreats to the house once again.
Recovered, he raises his gaze to the wall,
But no trace of cats can be seen there at all;
Till slowly but surely the shapes reappear.
Suddenly Buster begins to feel fear.

It's time, Morris reckons to negotiate,
He leaps from the wall and embraces his fate,
Confronting the dog in the yard face to face;
The cats hold their breath and bare claws just in case.
'We won't go away,' Morris sticks out his chin.
'We'll turn up each night, in the end you'll give in.
You'll go mad and get yourself beaten and kicked.
Your master will never know that he's been tricked.'

Wide-eyed and speechless, now Buster is made,
To listen to Morris's vengeful tirade,
Recounting each one of the brutal attacks,
That Buster has made on the neighbourhood's cats.
And as he concludes, something most strange occurs,
The puppy in Buster is reborn and stirs.
His big doleful eyes start to fill up with tears,
And he sobs as he tries to give voice to his fears.

'I'm sorry, I'm so sorry,' Buster proclaims,
Sobbing remorsefully as he explains,
How Syd Gutt would beat him and starve him until,
In a frenzy of fear he'd go in for the kill.
Convinced that sad Buster deserves to be seen,
As a victim of evil Syd Gutt's foul regime,
Mysterious Morris outlines his next plan,
Assuring him he will do all that he can.

Buster agrees straight away to the terms,
So, back to his anxious friends Morris returns.
Once on the wall, he gives Buster the nod,
And waits for Syd Gutt to feel destiny's prod.
As Buster starts barking, his master runs out,
Greeting his dog with a curse and a shout;
Then stops in his tracks at the sight of his hound,
Poised ready to pounce, crouching low to the ground.

Puzzled and terrified, Syd tries to run,
As Buster's huge jaws make a snap at his bum.
Then chaos and mayhem abound as the chase,
Hurtles upstairs and downstairs, all over the place.
In terror Syd screams as his pants lose their seat,
And Buster bites into a piece of raw meat.
This perfect diversion and terrible din,
Continue as Morris's friends all creep in.

Behind the front door, in a line three cats stand,
Bracing themselves for the next two to land,
On their backs that will form the next level to catch,
The sixth cat who'll be within reach of the latch.
The front door is opened, now Buster must run;
The cats howl the signal to tell him to come.
Upstairs where he's still in pursuit of his prey,
He leaves Syd Gutt quaking, this dog's had his day.

'Come on,' Morris shouts as the getaway's made,
Though Buster is with them, he's feeling afraid.
And as they get closer to Blackberry Drive,
He stops and starts wondering how he'll survive.
'I've had it,' he sighs when he's questioned by Mo.
'They'll hunt me and catch me, they won't let me go.'
'Don't worry,' says Morris, 'I've still got a plan.
Now, let's shift that collar as fast as we can.'

Paws, claws and teeth soon together release,
The thick studded collar in more than one piece.
Anonymous, Buster feels more than confused,
Shaking his head, he's completely bemused.
'Come on now,' says Morris, 'it's part of the ploy,
You're coming with me to meet Mrs Molloy.'
So, trusting in Morris's comforting tone,
Buster obediently follows him home.

In through the catflap slides Morris, alone,
As Buster's left waiting outside on his own.
His loud miaowing soon summons Mrs Molloy.
'Stop that noise Morris, you naughty big boy.'
But Morris jumps out through the catflap once more.
She follows and curiously opens the door.
'Good grief, Morris, who's this new friend
                you've brought round?'
She kneels to stroke Buster, who rolls on the ground.

Mrs Molloy invites Buster for tea.
She can't understand why this fine pedigree,
Is wearing no collar, nor owner's address;
How Morris acquired him she can't even guess.
And though she would help any creature in need,
A rottweiler's care is beyond her indeed.
But just at that moment she thinks of a man,
Who'll be able to help them if anyone can

Together the trio set off down the Drive,
To call on the Major at seventy-five.
An expert on canines, he's been on his own,
Since the death of his faithful old Labrador, Tone.
'Just leave him with me,' he tells Mrs Molloy.
'We'll find where you've come from, now won't we, old boy.
Now, you come inside since it's getting quite late.
We'll wait till tomorrow to investigate.'

Back in the comfort of Number Fifteen,
Mysterious Morris surveys the day's scheme,
While drifting to sleep on his cosy armchair,
As Mrs Molloy gently ruffles his fur.
Strange events followed at Buster's new home,
As day after day he was left there alone;
The Major out searching and asking around,
But from Buster's owner there wasn't a sound.

Weeks turned to months and then months to a year.
To Buster's delight it was made very clear,
That he'd been adopted, the Major would be,
His permanent owner indefinitely.
So, Morris's cats gained a valuable friend,
And Buster would prove to be loyal to the end.
And Morris was proved to be right once again,
By not rushing in to accuse and condemn.

....

Mysterious Morris

AND THE KIDNAP OF KITTEN JIM

In Blackberry Drive, at Number Fifteen,
A handsome grey cat can often be seen,
Asleep in the window, his head on his paws,
Contentedly curled, as dreaming, he snores;
Waiting for tea time and Mrs Molloy,
To call from the kitchen, 'Now where's my big boy?'
As she fills up his bowl right on four o' clock's chime,
The signal for Morris to rise and to shine.

Mysterious Morris comes blinking, awake.
He stretches and yawns, gives a sniff and a shake,
Emerging today from his usual dream,
Of turkey and salmon and lobster supreme.
When dinner is over he happily purrs,
Choosing which one of the cosy armchairs,
Upon which to settle and slumber away,
His huge dinner and the last hours of the day.

It's twilight when Morris slides down from the chair,
Then out through the catflap to find waiting there,
Black Burt who's come to see Mo for advice,
He sighs, wishing Burt had called round to chase mice.
'Do I sense a problem?' asks Morris, concerned.
'I'm not sure,' says Burt, 'but last evening I turned,
Up to meet Kitten Jim, as arranged, at nightfall,
I waited for hours, but no sign at all.'

'And when I went looking, it seems that Kit Jim,
Had missed lunch and dinner, and that's not like him.
I've asked everywhere, but it seems as I feared,
It looks as if Kit Jim has just disappeared.'
Morris falls silent, absorbing Burt's news.
Jim's just a kitten so he would not choose,
To go on the prowl for a night and a day.
It can only mean trouble that he's gone astray.

It's only a matter of weeks since Jim's been,
The new kitten living at Number Sixteen,
When Morris arranged for young Kit Jim to go,
Replacing the old, deceased Zanzibar Joe.
He's still far too small to be out on his own;
Mo nods, 'It's a moghunt,' in serious tone.
As if in reply, from on top of the shed,
A fur-covered teasel drops straight on Burt's head.

He springs up immediately on to the fence,
But whoever delivered this strange evidence,
Has vanished in seconds, so not to involve,
Himself in this mystery that Morris must solve.
'There's no doubt the fur comes from our Kitten Jim,
The colours are right and the scent is of him.'
But Morris detects something else with a sniff,
The foul scent of rats makes his whiskers go stiff.

'Doesn't look good,' he says, frowning at Burt,
Who's still on the lookout, crouched and alert.
'There's a mystery here, but if my guess is right,
Our friend Kitten Jim is in trouble tonight.'
That evening when darkness and silence descends,
A meeting takes place between Morris and friends.
There's Conker McGuinness and Footpad Magee,
And Algernon Flappit the tabby makes three.

Black Burt has left, to the ferals he's gone,
To tell them the search for Kit Jim is now on.
The friends try to work out the teasel's contents,
A sinister business that doesn't make sense.
Suddenly Algernon springs through the air,
And pounces on something he's seen moving there.
His extended paw and his claws rest upon,
A brown rat who, out of the sewers has come.

Algernon's snarling, preparing to bite,
But Morris shouts, 'Wait, for all we know he might,
Give us some information about Kitten Jim;
Remember the rat scent? It smelled just like him.'
So Algie backs off and they surround the rat,
Who, in Creaturespeak soon informs them all that,
He's there to deliver some important news,
A task he assures them that he did not choose.

'Speak up,' Morris growls, 'information or death.'
The rat trembles slightly then takes a deep breath.
'I sent to give message for Morris-cat-boss,
My Ratlord gives order that you come across,
To sewerland 'cos he got catbaby Jim.
If Morris not come, he make ratfood of him.
And, I not return by the break of the dawn,
Ratlord kill catbaby I told to warn.'

In rough creature language the rat then explains,
The Ratlord's intentions, his motives and aims.
It seems his demands are to do with the growth,
In the number of rats killed or eaten, or both,
By all of the feral cats living close by,
Since food has become very short in supply.
Resorting to hunting is desperate indeed,
But surviving starvation is their pressing need.

There's no trace of humour in Morris's laughter,
Dismissive contempt is the tone he is after.
'Your Ratlord thinks kidnapping our Kitten Jim,
And making a bargaining hostage of him,
Will stop the cats hunting for their food supply?
This Ratlord must know, if they did that they'd die.'
'Morris-cat-boss must tell Ratlord, not me,'
The rat smirks, now speaking quite confidently.

'If Morriscat not go to sewer with me,
Alone to meet Ratlord, then never you see,
Your cat baby Jim, he be killed and then ate.'
There's no choice for Morris, the trap's been well set.
Instructing the others to make no pursuit,
He follows the brown rat's circuitous route,
Into the sewers to hear the rat's terms.
Black Burt's in charge now until he returns.

Down into darkness now Morris descends,
Forsaking his safety as well as his friends.
Along fetid tunnels, through black night he crawls,
Past countless red eyes peering out from the walls.
The sewer of filth grows oppressively low,
Drenched in foul water, Mo's progress is slow.
Then, just when he feels that there's no journey's end,
There's suddenly light shining round the next bend.

From nowhere a cohort of rats now appears,
Forty or fifty, too many Mo fears,
To fight single-handed should something go wrong,
And claws are required to help justice along.
They usher him forward into a brick hall,
Whose roof drips black slime trickling down every wall.
And there on a platform, raised high from the rest,
The Ratlord reclines, calmly watching his guest.

'You very wise Morriscat come to my home.
Now we do business so you not alone,
When go back to outside with cat baby Jim;
But, you upset Ratlord, you ratfood for him.'
'Show me the kitten,' bold Morris calls out.
'First we make bargain,' the rat starts to shout.
'You stop all stray cats from my rats-kill-and-eat,
Then you take kitten back up to the street.'

Jim is brought in with a rat either side.
Mo gasps when he sees him, his eyes open wide.
His fur is all matted, he looks quite worn out;
Morris grows angry, preparing to shout.
Jim stands by the Ratlord whose face is a sneer.
'Jim,' Morris calls, 'don't you worry, I'm here.'
He bristles with rage, but the Ratlord can't see,
The peril he's in from his poised enemy.

'A curse on your ratpeople,' Morris proclaims,
'An exodus should be the first of your aims.
Lead them away before all of my cats,
Find out what's been done to Kit Jim by your rats.'
With one bound he stands on the platform beside,
The Ratlord, who instantly runs off to hide,
Shouting an order to kill the two cats.
Morris and Jim are encircled by rats.

'On to my back,' Morris calls, 'and hold tight.
Wrap your paws round me, we're in for a fight.'
Jim climbs aboard, safe on Morris's back,
As columns of rats all prepare to attack.
Now into the mob Morris plunges and roars,
Staking their lives on his four big strong paws.
Then, pushing and barging, his trial begins.
It's death for them both unless Morris wins.

In every direction the brown rats are thrown,
As Morris continues his last bid for home;
All the while pushing and crawling toward,
The daylight, away from the savage rat horde.
Heaving and shoving, he keeps forging on,
He knows if he stops then all hope will be gone.
But the burden of Jim, and the ferocious fight,
Are taking their toll on brave Morris's might.

Although there's a glimmer of daylight ahead,
He turns to Kit Jim sadly shaking his head.
'There's too many of them, I can't carry on.
Run for the entrance, I'll do what I can.'
Then, roaring with rage he does not hesitate,
He turns on the rat horde, embracing his fate.
Jim bids for freedom and runs for the light,
While Morris is left to continue the fight.

Blindly Jim runs, daring not to look back,
Terrified that he's still under attack.
But, just as the rats bring Mo down to the ground,
From not far away comes a different sound.
A furious howling as Burt's gang of mogs,
Comes hurtling into the rats like war's dogs.
The rats flee in panic with cats giving chase,
As Burt turns to Morris, a grin on his face.

'Thought you might just need a hand to get out.
Kit Jim is fine, come on, don't hang about.'
Back in the daylight the friends reunite,
For sore eyes the sunshine's a wonderful sight.
With Jim safely home, all the friends take their leave;
Next morning they all find it hard to believe,
When a message arrives from the Ratlord to say,
His rat horde is leaving, they're going away.

Mysterious Morris returns to his chair,
Intending to spend quite some time dozing there.
But mysteries come and mysteries go,
Their timing is guesswork, and wouldn't you know,
The very next day Morris goes out to find,
A message from Burt asking if he would mind,
Looking into a problem that simply won't keep.
Sighing and nodding, he goes back to sleep.

....

Mysterious Morris

AND THE BLACKBERRY DRIVE BURGLARS

Mysterious Morris climbs down from the chair,
And pads to the kitchen to find waiting there,
A bowl that's half empty, as Mrs Molloy,
Calls, 'Time for your diet, my big hungry boy.
Oh, stop it, don't give me that miserable stare,
You know what the vet said, last time we were there,
That if you continue to fill up your face,
You'll soon be a big, fat, grey, furry disgrace.'

Less than convinced by this wretched advice,
Mysterious Morris knows hunger's the price,
That he'll just have to pay to get back into shape,
For Mrs Molloy and her measuring tape.
And later that night, when it's time to go out,
To meet with his friends who are prowling about,
He can't help but notice that recently he's,
Now finding the cat flap a bit of a squeeze.

There's somebody already waiting outside,
As Morris appears first to ooze and then glide,
Outward, provoking an unkind response,
From Black Burt who's quick to remind Mo that once,
He could zip through the cat flap, not touching the sides,
'Well, I've gone on a diet,' cross Morris replies.
'Now, if you don't mind, can we leave it alone.'
Burt grins, but respects Mo's irascible tone.

'Any more news on that burglary yet?'
Asks Morris, 'I thought they'd have managed to get,
The offender by now since it's already been,
A week since the break-in at Number Nineteen.'
'To make matters worse,' answers Burt, 'I've just learned,
It seems that the burglars must have returned,
Since Kitten Jim's house was done over last night.
It gave poor Jim's owner a terrible fright.'

'So, that means both victims are old ladies who,
Live alone with their cats, don't you think that's a clue?'
'Of course,' answers Burt, 'it would seem to make sense,
They're picking on those who've no means of defence.'
'Cowardly actions and mischief afoot!
A case that stands open, a case we must shut.
Keep asking questions while I make a plan.
I'll meet with the others as soon as I can.'

The following night, just as Morris had said,
A meeting takes place in the old garden shed.
There's Conker McGuinness and Footpad Magee,
And Algernon Flappit the tabby makes three.
Once they're assembled, it's not long before,
Burt rushes in with fresh news of some more,
Nasty break-ins, all down at the old people's flats,
Where old ladies live on their own with their cats.

'Time we looked after our owners' interests,'
Says Morris, 'Let's track down these unwelcome guests.
I've got an idea, it really depends,
On cooperation from all of our friends.'
So, five cats set off to pay visits and calls,
To set up a vigil for after night falls.
Soon, on every rooftop, though no one would know,
A cat watches over the dark streets below.

It's just after two when the burglars arrive,
Parking their white van in Blackberry Drive.
Shadowy figures emerge from inside,
Furtively moving, their presence to hide.
But from high above a sharp lookout observes,
Then howls out the signal, which jangles their nerves.
'Cats give me the creeps,' shudders one of the men,
Notorious housebreaker, Light-fingered Len.

'I hate 'em meself,' says Len's mate, Barry Spears,
Pulling his woolly hat over his ears.
While high on the rooftops each cat spies upon,
The robbers' next move before passing it on,
To Morris who waits with his faithful mogband,
Ready to lend a bit more than fate's hand.
They're ready to move when the message comes through,
That Barry and Len are outside Number Two.

The house is in darkness so neither man sees,
Three cats creeping stealthily out from the trees.
Algernon Flappit and Footpad Magee,
Both slip through the cat flap then turn anxiously,
To see meaty Morris half in and half out,
Stuck fast in the cat flap, not daring to shout.
'Get on with the plan,' Morris pants urgently,
'I'll just have to hope that they don't notice me.'

Algie and Footpad leave Morris behind,
As Barry and Len reach reach the back door to find,
The cat flap is blocked by a furry backside,
As Morris's front half hangs hidden inside.
'That's odd,' observes Barry, 'but I'm pretty sure,
There's a great big cat's bum hanging out of this door.'
'Well shift it,' says Len, 'it'll have to come out,
We can't get inside, go on, give it a clout.'

So Barry walks back, preparing his run,
To deliver a jolly good kick up the bum,
While inside a grimacing Morris begins,
To regret the results of his gluttonous sins.
A pounding approach and a thumping left boot,
Gives Morris the impetus he needs to shoot,
Like a rocket, vacating the hole in the door,
To make a crash-landing on the kitchen floor.

'That does it,' he scowls. 'They really will pay.
There'll be no more burglaries after today.'
So, gingerly making his way up the stairs,
Mysterious Morris surveys then prepares,
A special reception for Barry and Len,
Who make their forced entry in silence and then,
Creep stealthily through from the kitchen and pause,
While upstairs the old lady peacefully snores.

Up on the landing, the cats leave no trace,
Concealing themselves as the break-in takes place;
Silently poised at the top of the stairs,
Ready to end these dishonest affairs.
The light switch is covered by Algernon's paw,
As Morris and Footpad keep low to the floor.
They're well out of sight as the men start to climb,
Upward, in darkness, they're wasting no time.

Soon, from the bedroom they sneak with their swag,
They've just helped themselves to the lady's handbag.
Time then for action as Mo gives a shout,
Like lightning both Footpad and he now shoot out,
Placing themselves on the very top stair,
Just at the moment Len's foot arrives there.
Tripping then wobbling, Len's arms start to flail,
He falls down the stairs on his way back to gaol.

The plan's going well, and in no time at all,
Algernon's paw hits the switch on the wall.
Barry gawps down at an unconscious Len,
He dashes downstairs, just ignores him and then,
He's off through the backdoor and over the fence,
Forgetting the valuable handbag's contents.
In seconds he reaches the van and jumps in,
To find himself faced with a Cheshire cat's grin.

Conker McGuinness sits blocking the view,
Outside on the bonnet. 'Get off, I'll 'ave you,'
Roars Barry, but Conker just sits there and smirks,
Desperately hoping the plan really works.
On cue comes Black Burt dashing in from the side,
The signal for Conker to run off and hide,
As furious Barry jumps out of the van,
Intending to batter the cat if he can.

But Conker makes haste and is safe in the trees,
As from the ignition, Burt snatches the keys.
Poor Barry returns to be faced with the sight,
Of a cat with a mouthful of keys in full flight.
'It's not fair,' he whinges while stamping both feet.
The sound of a siren is heard in the street.
Police cars and neighbours are soon on the scene;
Len is arrested and Barry comes clean.

Already Mo's band of adventuring friends,
Is far from the scene as the night's drama ends;
Leaving the old lady from Number Two,
Quite safe in her bed, although she never knew,
Protection had come from a feline defence,
And not from the burglars' own incompetence.
So Morris goes home with his huge appetite,
To find his short rations a miserable sight.

But then he thinks back and recalls with a wince,
The boot up the cat flap that helped to convince,
Him that Mrs Molloy had been right all along,
Insisting his excessive eating was wrong.
'It's doing you good,' she encourages Mo,
But Mrs Molloy couldn't possibly know,
The reason why Morris is looking so glum,
Is, he still finds it painful to sit on his bum.

....

Lightning Source UK Ltd.
Milton Keynes UK
18 June 2010
155787UK00001B/26/P

9 781452 018096